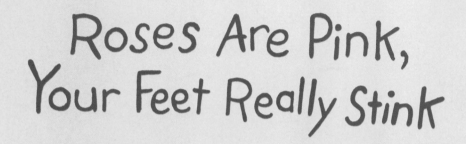

Roses Are Pink,
Your Feet Really Stink

Roses Are Pink, Your Feet Really Stink

Diane de Groat

Morrow Junior Books / New York

Watercolors were used for the full-color illustrations.
The text type is 14-point Korinna.

8 9 10
Library of Congress Cataloging-in-Publication Data

DeGroat, Diane.
Roses are pink, your feet really stink / Diane deGroat.
p. cm.
Summary: On Valentine's Day, Gilbert brings a tin of homemade cookies and his
original nice or nasty poems to school.
ISBN 0-688-13604-4 (trade)—ISBN 0-688-13605-2 (library)—ISBN 0-688-15220-1 (pbk.)
[1. Valentine's Day—Fiction. 2. Valentines—Fiction.] I. Title. PZ7.D3639Ro 1996
[E]—dc20 94-43773 CIP AC

Violets are blue;
Roses are red.
—To children's
librarians!
'Nuf said.

— D.d.

There they were, fifteen blank valentine cards waiting to be filled with nice valentine poems. They were sitting on the kitchen table in a pile as high as Gilbert's nose. Mrs. Byrd had told them to write something nice for each classmate, because Valentine's Day was about liking each other.

Gilbert liked Patty a lot. She had smiley eyes and a silly laugh that made Gilbert feel silly, too. He picked out the biggest card and wrote inside:

Roses are red,
violets are blue.
Your eyes are nice,
and I like you.

Gilbert

Gilbert also liked Frank. Frank let Gilbert use his baseball mitt once when Gilbert forgot to bring his own. On Frank's card, he wrote:

Your name is Frank.
It isn't Hank.
You lent me your mitt,
so you I thank.

Gilbert

This is fun, Gilbert thought. He continued to write nice valentine poems until there were two cards left. One for Lewis and one for Margaret.

Gilbert didn't want to write a nice poem for Lewis. Lewis once tweaked Gilbert's nose until it turned red.

He didn't want to write a nice poem for Margaret, either. Margaret made fun of Gilbert's glasses.

...So he didn't write nice poems.

On Lewis's card he wrote:

Violets are blue, roses are pink. Your feet are big, and they really stink.

Gilbert thought the poem was funny, but maybe Lewis wouldn't. Maybe he would tweak Gilbert's nose when he read it! Gilbert didn't want Lewis to tweak his nose again, so he didn't sign his name. He signed it... "Margaret."

On Margaret's card he wrote:

Roses are red,
you wet your bed.
I think that you
have rocks in your
head.

Gilbert liked the poem, but he didn't think
Margaret would. He didn't want Margaret to
say mean things to him again, so he signed
the card..."Lewis."

On Valentine's Day, Gilbert walked to school with fifteen cards and a tin of valentine cookies that his mother had baked for the party.

Mrs. Byrd let everyone open their cards. One of Gilbert's cards had X's all over the envelope, so he opened it first. It said:

Roses are red, violets are blue. You are my friend, and I like you.

X X X X

It was signed "Patty." Gilbert smiled at Patty and Patty giggled back.

Gilbert opened the rest of his cards. They were all very friendly. Even Lewis had written a poem for him:

You may be small.
You're not very tall.
But I like the way
that you play ball.
Lewis

Gilbert was happy that Lewis liked the way he played ball. And Margaret wrote:

Sometimes you are
very sweet.
I hope you brought
nice cookies to eat.

love,
Margaret

Gilbert smiled to himself. Margaret thought that he was very sweet! He looked over at Margaret. She wasn't happy with one of her valentines.

She stuck her tongue out at Lewis. Lewis wasn't happy with one of his valentines, either. He stuck his tongue out at Margaret. Margaret pushed Lewis. Lewis called Margaret a bad name.

Party: 2:00

Mrs. Byrd said, "Quiet, please! Valentine's Day is about liking each other, not about fighting." She made the class do workbooks for the rest of the morning. Everyone was mad at Lewis and Margaret. Even Gilbert.

When it was reading time, Margaret looked through all of her valentines again and said, "I have two valentines from Lewis—a good one and a bad one."

Lewis said, "I didn't write a bad one. Someone else wrote my name." He looked through his own pile of cards and said, "I have two valentines from Margaret, and none from Gilbert!" Then he shouted, "Oh, no! Gilbert wrote the bad cards and signed our names!"

And Mrs. Byrd said, "Quiet, please!"

At lunch, nobody wanted to sit near Gilbert. Not even
Patty. He had to sit all by himself. When he peeked over his
carrot-and-banana sandwich, he could see Patty and Lewis
giggling at their table.

Gilbert wondered if Lewis thought Patty had smiley eyes and a silly laugh, too. He saw Margaret eating a peanut-butter-and-jelly sandwich like she did every day. Gilbert liked peanut-butter-and-jelly sandwiches and wished that he was eating one, too.

At recess, nobody played with Gilbert, and Gilbert was
very sorry that he had written two mean and nasty valentines.

When they all lined up to go inside, Patty finally asked, "Why did you write bad things about your friends, Gilbert?"

"Because Lewis tweaked my nose," Gilbert said. "And Margaret made fun of my glasses."

Lewis said, "I'm sorry I tweaked your nose, Gilbert. You can tweak mine if you want." Gilbert gave Lewis's nose a little tweak, but it didn't turn red.

And Margaret said, "I'm sorry I made fun of your glasses, Gilbert. I will wear them for the rest of the day." She put on Gilbert's glasses, but she couldn't see anything, and Gilbert couldn't see anything, so she gave them back.

In art class, Gilbert made two new
valentines out of red paper and lace.

During spelling, Gilbert wrote a new poem for Lewis:

Violets are blue,
roses are pink.
I'm sorry I said that
your feet really stink.

Then Gilbert thought of something nice about Margaret. He liked the way that she always smelled like peanut butter and jelly, so he wrote a new poem for her:

Roses are red.
Jelly is sweet.
You smell as good
as the sandwich
you eat.

Then, in math, Gilbert figured out that he had 364 days
before he would have to write any more valentines!

Finally it was time for the party. Gilbert gave the new cards to Lewis and Margaret, and he passed out the cookies that his mother had baked.

And each cookie said: